THE FROST RONA
WALKER'S WOLF

THE UNOFFICIAL ANIMAL WARRIORS
OF THE OVERWORLD SERIES

THE FROST
WALKER'S WOLF

AN UNOFFICIAL MINECRAFTERS NOVEL

BOOK ONE

Maya Grace

Sky Pony Press
New York

THE UNOFFICIAL ANIMAL WARRIORS OF THE OVERWORLD SERIES: THE FROST WALKER'S WOLF.

Copyright © 2019 by Hollan Publishing, Inc.

Minecraft® is a registered trademark of Notch Development AB.

The Minecraft game is copyright © Mojang AB.

All rights reserved. No part of this book may be reproduced in any manner without the express written consent of the publisher, except in the case of brief excerpts in critical reviews or articles. All inquiries should be addressed to Sky Pony Press, 307 West 36th Street, 11th Floor, New York, NY 10018.

Sky Pony Press books may be purchased in bulk at special discounts for sales promotion, corporate gifts, fund-raising, or educational purposes. Special editions can also be created to specifications. For details, contact the Special Sales Department, Sky Pony Press, 307 West 36th Street, 11th Floor, New York, NY 10018 or info@skyhorsepublishing.com.

Sky Pony® is a registered trademark of Skyhorse Publishing, Inc.®, a Delaware corporation.

Visit our website at www.skyponypress.com.

10 9 8 7 6 5 4 3 2 1

Library of Congress Cataloging-in-Publication Data is available on file.

Special thanks to Erin L. Falligant.

Cover illustration by Amanda Brack
Cover design by Brian Peterson

Paperback ISBN: 978-1-5107-4133-1
Ebook ISBN: 978-1-5107-4138-6

Printed in Canada

TABLE OF CONTENTS

CHAPTER 1

The Art of Growing Nether Wart: Potion Brewing for Beginners: The Super-Charged Creeper (and Other Cautionary Tales. Ella slid her finger along the worn book spines lining Gran's bookcase. *It doesn't matter which book I choose,* she reminded herself. *What matters is the enchantment I get!*

She grabbed the Nether wart book and slid it into the left-hand slot of the enchantment table. Then she reached into the bin for a piece of lapis lazuli. The blue stone felt cool and smooth beneath her fingertips.

"Okay," she said out loud. "Here goes nothing."

She plunked the lapis lazuli into the right-hand slot of the enchantment table. Then she stared at the thick book with the golden cover that rested atop the table. As if a breeze had blown through the drafty room, the pages of the book began to flutter. Sparks flew between that thick, golden book and the scads of other books on the shelves surrounding the enchantment table. Ella inhaled deeply, wishing she could breathe in all of that magic and knowledge and keep it for herself. But as soon as it had begun, the moment—and magic— passed. The only remnant was the mysterious purple glow of the book she had placed in the slot.

Ella slid it out carefully, as if it might be hot to the touch. Then she dropped it with a sigh.

"Depth Strider." She practically spit the words. What good was the Depth Strider enchantment when she lived at the top of a hill, far away from lakes, rivers, and mountain streams? The only body of water nearby was the tiny fishpond Gran had dug for her cousin Jack. Ella didn't need to wear Depth Strider boots to swim across that pond. She could pretty much *leap* across it in a single bound.

"Save it for later," she told herself, tossing the enchanted book on the bottom shelf alongside all the other books with useless enchantments.

Gran said they might be useful *someday,* and she had taught Ella how to use an anvil to transfer those enchantments onto tools and other things.

"Someday," Ella said thoughtfully. "I'm going to hold you to that, Gran."

She checked the clock on the wall, which showed the sun dipping low in the circular sky. She had time for one more enchantment before dinner. But as she reached for another book, Ella froze. A faint howling— the same sound that had woken her up that morning— pricked her ears. She cocked her head, straining to hear.

What *was* that?

Was Jack crying out from the basement, like he had the day he'd tripped and broken all of his potion bottles? No. This sound wasn't quite human. Was it a mob—the dreaded moan of the zombies Gran had warned Ella and her cousins about? Maybe. But the sound wasn't scary exactly. It was more . . . sad. Terribly, awfully sad.

Ella pulled the hood of her cape up over her ears. The thick wool muffled the mournful sound. So did the chime of the bell tower—Gran's signal that dinner was about to be served. *Thank goodness!* thought Ella. Something about the strange howling made her long to be with Gran and her cousins, to be safe and snug in a warm kitchen rather than alone in the drafty enchantment room.

She closed the glass doors of the fireplace and raced down the long, winding hall that led past the crafting room. Around this corner and that, her heeled boots clattered with every step—until she hit the soft woven rug. As she rounded the hallway toward the kitchen, she paused to enjoy the sunset. Well, it wasn't a *real* sunset. It was a canvas painting of mountains cast in the purple glow of the fading sun.

Gran's rule was to slow down enough to appreciate *one* beautiful thing every day. She'd be asking the kids about it at dinner—Ella knew to be prepared. Then she raced down the last twisty hall toward the kitchen. Screeched to a halt. Sighed. And backed up a few steps toward the basement door. Gran's other rule was to never leave Jack behind. Even at dinnertime, it was Ella's job to find him and make sure he'd heard the bell. There was *nothing* wrong with Jack's hearing. But when a boy spends all his time brewing potions in the basement, he's bound to miss something. *So why is that* my *problem?* thought Ella as she started down the cobblestone steps.

She wound around the circular staircase, dodging cobwebs and tripping over mossy stones.

"Jack!" she called into the darkness. Gran kept torches going at all hours—that was one more rule of hers. But the thick obsidian walls of the basement seemed to suck the light right out of those torches.

At the base of the stairs, Ella felt for the handle of the heavy oak door. She pushed it open with a grunt. There was Jack, bent over the brewing stand, a tuft of his wayward hair poking out over the top. He glanced up, squinting into the light. "What?" he said.

"Dinner!" said Ella. "Gran already rang the bell."

She turned to start back up the staircase. She could smell the fresh bread Gran had just pulled from the oven. She could practically *taste* it. But the potion bubbling on Jack's brewing stand was such an unusual shade of lavender-blue that she snuck another look. "Is that a new one?" she asked.

He stood a bit taller. "Potion of swiftness," he announced. "Gran harvested some sugar cane for me."

"Good old Gran," said Ella.

Gran grew *everything* in her garden, from tall stalks of golden wheat to dewy melons and plump pumpkins.

And if she'd harvested sugar cane, there'd be pumpkin pie for dinner. Yum!

Ella took the stairs two by two, until a silverfish scuttled across her path. "Yuck!" She dodged the critter, then carefully navigated the last few steps until she'd made it to the top.

She heard music drifting from the kitchen before she even stepped foot inside. Gran had an old jukebox that she played round the clock, filling the room with sweet melodies.

As Ella entered, Gran glanced up from the table she was setting. Her silver hair spilled down over her cyan-colored robe—just one of the many shades of blue lining her closet. "There's my girl," said Gran with a warm smile. She was almost *always* smiling. But Ella knew that behind Gran's grey eyes lay a great well of sadness, too. She gave Gran a squeeze just as Jack trotted into the room. But their oldest cousin, Rowan, was missing.

"Will you find her, please?" asked Gran, giving Ella a knowing look.

Ella fought the urge to roll her eyes. *Why do I have to be the messenger? I'm starving!* But she would never say something like that to Gran. Not after everything Gran had done for her and her cousins.

Ella jogged through the kitchen, toward the front of the house. It was more like a mansion really. Gran's house had twenty-three rooms—Ella and Jack had counted them one day. Bedrooms, crafting rooms, an enchantment room, a potion-brewing room . . . But not one of them was interesting enough to keep Rowan inside for long.

Ella pushed through the front door and skipped down the stone steps.

"Hey, Golem!" she shouted through the gate. "Seen Rowan anywhere?"

The enormous iron golem spun his head to gaze at her, his eyes dark and watchful beneath his heavy brow. He clanked toward the gate and held out a long arm, magically producing a rose. But he said nothing, as usual.

"Aw, thanks," said Ella, reaching for the rose.

She broke off the stem and tucked the rose behind her ear. Then she began her nightly game of Hide and Seek with Rowan. Was her cousin perched on the obsidian wall circling the mansion? Hanging out her bedroom window at the top of the turret? Dangling her feet over the edge of the rooftop? Ella spun in a slow circle, looking up. As the sun slid behind a cloud, she shivered—and heard the *click* of the beacon lighting up behind her. The mansion grounds would never fall dark. Gran made sure of that.

"Blast! Why is that thing so bright?"

Ella turned to see Rowan straddling the wall, dressed in black from head to toe. If not for her fiery red ponytail, she would have blended right in with the dark stone.

"I can see clear to the extreme hills," said Rowan, pointing. "At least I could, until that beacon blinded me."

She was always scanning the horizon, searching for something. *But what?* wondered Ella. *Does she wish she could sprout wings and fly away? Leave us all behind?* Ella's heart ached at the thought.

"Come up here and look!" said Rowan.

Ella eyed the spindly vine ladder strung over the wall. "No, thanks."

Rowan shot her a glance. "Don't you want to see what's out there? Aren't you even kind of curious?"

Ella shook her head. "I know what's out there—zombies, skeletons, spider jockeys, Endermen . . ."

Rowan snorted. "Gran sure has you spooked. She's teaching you to be a scaredy-cat."

Hot lava bubbled up in Ella's chest. "No she's not! She's *teaching* me how to do enchantments. She's teaching Jack how to brew potions. And she'd teach you a few things too, if you'd let her."

Rowan clamped her mouth shut. She stared back out over the horizon, inching forward along the wall.

"Why do you care so much about the world outside these walls?" asked Ella, her voice cracking. "Don't we have everything we need here? Gran loves us and protects us . . ."

Rowan kicked at the stone with her heel. "I don't need protection," she spat. "I'd rather go out there and see the Overworld, like our parents did."

Ella swallowed hard. As the sun made its final descent, she allowed herself to think about her mother—but only for a moment. She and her cousins lived with Gran because their parents had died during the Uprising, when the day and night cycle stopped and hostile mobs spawned uncontrollably across the Overworld.

Gran rarely spoke of the children she had lost, but Ella longed to know, *Am I like my mother? Am I brave like she was?*

A low, pitiful howl suddenly pierced the silence.

Ella whirled around. Was it a dog? Or . . . a wolf? She glanced at Rowan to see if she had heard, but her cousin sat perfectly still, staring out over the horizon.

"Did you . . . ?" Ella's question trailed off. If she asked Rowan about wolves, her cousin would just call her a scaredy-cat again, or go off on Gran for filling her head with spooky thoughts.

So Ella said nothing.

But a trickle of worry ran down her spine. The howling was growing louder, more insistent. And instead of trying to figure out what it was, Ella wanted to run inside and hide—to bury herself in Gran's robes and shut her ears to the world outside.

I'm not brave like my mother, she decided, forcing back hot tears. *But Rowan is.*

CHAPTER 2

Ella could see the grey wolf pacing, hear it panting, feel its fear. Its golden eyes pleaded with her through the darkness, begging for help. When he raised his head toward the night sky, she braced herself for the sound—for the howl that woke her with a start and sent her tumbling out of bed.

"Ouch!"

The bedroom door creaked open, sending another wave of fear through Ella.

But it was only Jack, rubbing his eyes. "Why were you hollering?" he asked. "Wait, why are you on the floor?"

Ella scrambled to stand, but tripped in the tangled sheets. "Just a nightmare," she said quickly. "I thought I saw—I mean, *heard* a . . ."

"Heard what?"

Can I trust him? Ella wondered.

Jack wouldn't accuse her of being scared, like Rowan had. So Ella let the words tumble out. "I thought I heard a wolf. Did you hear it too?"

Jack shook his head. "But I heard the breakfast bell." He sounded proud, as if it might be his day's most impressive accomplishment.

"Good for you," said Ella with a grin. "I'll meet you down there."

After Jack left, she carefully untangled herself from the sheets. Then she listened for a few seconds longer. Was the wolf real? Or just a bad dream?

She shook her head and pulled her hood up over her ears. If he called to her again, she wasn't sure she wanted to hear it.

* * *

"Jack, wipe your mouth." Ella handed him a napkin.

"Mind your own breakfast," Gran scolded. "You've barely touched it."

But Ella couldn't eat a bite. She couldn't shake the sense of dread that had followed her out of bed, down the stairs, and into the kitchen. *What's wrong with me?* she wondered, sliding the melon around in her bowl.

As soon as Gran left the kitchen, Rowan leaned closer. "What's going on with you?" she whispered.

Ella shrugged. She sure wasn't going to spill the details of her dream to Rowan.

"She had a nightmare," piped up Jack. "About wolves."

"Jack, be quiet!" Ella snapped. "And wipe your face already."

But the damage was done.

Rowan cocked her head. "Wolves?" she asked. "Are you hearing wolves?"

Her expression was so strange. *Does she hear it too?* Ella wondered, biting her lip. *Why else would she ask me that?*

"You *do* hear them!" said Rowan, slapping her hand on the table. "I knew it."

"I don't!" said Jack, sounding envious.

Ella grabbed Rowan's arm. "You know about them? Why didn't you say something? Where is the sound coming from?" Suddenly, she wanted to know everything. She pushed her hood off her ears and stared at Rowan, waiting.

Rowan raised a finger to her lips. "Not here," she whispered. "Let's go out back."

"Me too!" said Jack.

But Ella cut him off at the pass. "I need you to brew us a potion," she said. "Let's see . . . how about potion of night vision?"

A smile spread slowly across Jack's face. "I have carrots," he said. "But not *golden* carrots. I need gold nuggets to make those."

Ella sighed. "I'll look for some in my chest," she said. "Go see if you have everything else you need, okay?"

Jack took off from the table like a shot.

"Nice work," said Rowan.

But Ella didn't need compliments. What she *needed* were answers. So she followed her cousin through the dining room, across the living room, and out the back door.

Gran was weeding the garden, so the girls wound around the pond to the other side of the yard.

"Okay," said Ella. "Tell me about the wolves."

Rowan shook her head. "I'm not going to tell you. I'm going to *show* you."

As she headed toward the wall and reached for the vine ladder, Ella's stomach sunk. But now was no time for fear. If she had to scale that wall to get some answers out of Rowan, she would.

The vines burned the palms of her hands, and it took Ella twice as long to get to the top as it had Rowan. But finally she was high enough to swing her leg over the wall.

As the world swayed beneath her, she gripped the stones and hung on for dear life. "We're practically in the clouds," she whispered, trying not to look down.

"You'll get used to it," said Rowan, laughing. "Now look over there."

She pointed north, past the village at the base of the hill, past the expanse of plains, past the dense forest, all the way to the snowcapped tops of the extreme hills.

"The wolves live in the forest," she said. "And in the Taiga beyond."

Ella strained her eyes, as if she might be able to make out the wolf's face from so many miles away.

"He's in danger," she said suddenly, remembering her dream. "My wolf is in danger."

"*Your* wolf?" said Rowan.

"The one who's calling to me," said Ella, trying to explain. "He needs my help."

Rowan blew out her breath. "I've heard the wolves too," she said. "But I didn't know you had your own."

Ella waited for Rowan to tease her or accuse her of making the whole thing up. But she didn't. Instead, she faced Ella straight on. "Do you want to help him?"

"Yes! But I don't know how." As she spoke, she fought back tears.

"Well, maybe he'll tell you how," said Rowan solemnly. "If you listen."

Together, the girls turned toward the Taiga, waiting. But the only sound Ella heard was Jack, calling to her from the back porch—asking her for more gold nuggets.

If only helping my wolf were as easy as helping Jack with his potion, she thought sadly.

Then she swung her leg back over the wall and started the slow trek down.

CHAPTER 3

The wolf led her through the forest, turning back every few steps to make sure she followed. He panted and whined as if to say, *Hurry up! Go faster! Follow me!* But Ella couldn't run faster. She kept tripping over tree roots and twigs scattered along the forest trail.

Suddenly, the woods gave way to a rocky mountain, so steep that Ella had to use her hands to climb. She inched upward, following the silver tail that kept disappearing along the ledges above.

Then the stones turned to ice. Ella shivered, her body aching with cold. But she followed her wolf through the icy plains.

He stopped suddenly and turned, growling. Fear flooded Ella's chest, until she realized he wasn't growling at her. There was something *behind* her.

She heard the grunting and felt hot breath on her neck. Then the mobs behind her started to run. She heard their footsteps, but her own feet wouldn't budge.

Her wolf crouched low, preparing to fight—to protect her against the hostile mobs.

"No!" she hollered. "Go! Run!" Because as much as the wolf wanted to protect her, she wanted to protect *him*. "Run!"

Something grabbed her from behind. She flailed her arms and fought to free herself—until she heard Gran's soothing voice.

"Ella! It's alright, dear. It's just a dream."

Ella's eyes flung open, and there was Gran, leaning over her with a concerned smile. "It was just a dream," she said again. "A bad dream. All better now?" She tenderly tucked a strand of Ella's hair behind her ear.

Ella nodded, but her heart thumped in her ears. *Don't tell Gran about the wolf,* she told herself. *Not a word.*

She couldn't tell Gran about the wolf, because the wolf was pleading with her to leave the safety of the walled mansion. And Gran would never allow that. *Not ever,* thought Ella.

A low, mournful howl rose from the hills outside her window. Could Gran hear it, too? Ella watched her face carefully, but saw nothing—not a single flicker of emotion.

Gran doesn't hear it, Ella decided. *So she won't understand it.*

When Gran asked again if Ella was "all better now," she nodded and forced a smile. Whatever was going on with her wolf, she and Rowan would have to figure it out—on their own.

* * *

"He wanted me to follow him," Ella said in hushed tones. "He showed me the way."

Rowan nodded solemnly. "Through the forest, to the Taiga."

The girls sat in the enchantment room with the door closed. Even with flames flickering in the fireplace, Ella shivered. "He's in danger," she said, her voice rising. "Something's after him—destroying his pack. We have to help!"

"Then we'll have to go," said Rowan, her eyes flashing. She brushed her gloved hands together and stood up, as if she were ready to leave that instant.

"But how?" said Ella. "We don't know the way to the Taiga. We don't have any weapons. If we run into hostile mobs, we won't be able to save the wolves. We won't even be able to save ourselves!"

Rowan held out her hand. "Follow me."

Ella's heart fluttered. "Where?"

Rowan led the way down the hall, past the crafting room. She walked with long, purposeful strides, and Ella had to jog to keep up with her.

"Where are we going?" Ella asked again.

But Rowan kept walking. After zigzagging down two hallways and then a third, she stopped and held a finger to her lips.

They were almost to the kitchen now, where Gran was making applesauce. Ella heard the clinking of glass jars and Gran's sweet voice floating over the music disc playing in the jukebox.

But instead of entering the kitchen, Rowan pointed toward the wall, to the painting of the sunset.

"Yeah, so?" whispered Ella. It seemed a strange time to stop and appreciate something beautiful. What was Rowan thinking?

Then Ella watched in disbelief as Rowan lifted the corner of the canvas. She peeled it back slowly. Beneath the hanging canvas, Ella saw . . .

. . . a *door*.

"What—?" she started to say.

Rowan clamped her hand over Ella's mouth. She nodded toward the door as if to say, "Just come see." Then she pushed the door inward.

It creaked a little, enough to make Ella's heart thump in her ears. Had Gran heard?

No. Gran was still humming in the kitchen.

So Ella followed Rowan into the darkness. As Rowan rubbed flint against steel, sparks flew. She lit a torch, revealing the contents of the secret room.

Ella sucked in her breath.

The room held *weapons*—lots of them. Iron swords lined the walls. Bows hung from hooks, above bucketfuls of arrows. As Ella's eyes adjusted, she saw piles of armor, too. Chestplates were stacked like saddles. Helmets rested beneath them like dead silverfish, belly up.

"What is all this?" Ella asked, her voice cracking. "Is it Gran's?" She couldn't picture her grandma wearing armor over her soft robes, or holding a sword in her hand instead of a garden hoe.

Rowan shrugged. "Judging by the dust and cobwebs, nothing in here has been used since the Uprising. I mean, except for a bow I snuck out when I first found this place."

The Uprising. Ella's throat tightened. Had her mother used these weapons? Was she wearing any of this armor when she'd been killed?

"So we have weapons," said Rowan. "And we can get a map in the village." She said it so casually, as if she were going to trade for milk and eggs at the village market.

As the sound of Gran's humming floated through the cracked door, Ella winced. "We can't leave Gran," she whispered.

"Well, we can't take her with us," Rowan countered. "She needs to stay here and look after Jack. And if we tell her, well . . ."

Ella sighed. "I know. She won't let us go."

In the shadows of the tiny room, she again saw her wolf's face. She heard his terrified panting, and remembered the way he had leaped to her defense as hostile mobs approached.

How can I not go? she asked herself. *I have to save him, if I can!*

CHAPTER 4

Ella slid an iron sword into the slot of the anvil, and an enchanted book into the other slot.

Clink, clink, clink!

"Shh!" said Rowan, who stood lookout at the door of the garden shed.

"I can't help it!" said Ella. "Did he hear?"

Rowan snuck another peek at Jack, who was fishing in the pond. "Nah. He's totally into his pufferfish."

Gran had stocked the pond with fish so that Jack could catch them for his potions. *Good old Gran*, Ella thought again. Gran took such good care of them—all of them. *And Rowan and I are going to break her heart when we go.*

But the plan was in motion now—there was no turning back.

Every night for the past week, Ella and Rowan had snuck weapons and armor into the garden shed, where Gran kept an anvil. Ella had lugged armfuls of enchanted books down, too. And whenever the coast was clear—when Gran wasn't within earshot—Ella had used the anvil to transfer enchantments from the books onto other things.

All of those useless enchantments that Ella had been saving for "someday," like Depth Strider, Flame, and Protection, suddenly seemed *very* useful. Necessary, in fact.

Clink, clink, clink!

She enchanted two sets of armor with Protection. Then she enchanted Rowan's boots with Depth Strider. *Because she's a better swimmer than me,* thought Ella. With any luck, she wouldn't have to do any swimming in the Taiga.

She gave the Sharpness enchantment to Rowan's sword, and Fire Aspect to her own. *I don't want to fight with a sword,* thought Ella, *but maybe I can cook with it.* Fire Aspect would set anything she touched on fire. At the thought of blackened salmon, her mouth watered.

"Should we bring one of Jack's fishing poles?" she whispered.

Rowan nodded. "Good idea. Can you enchant it with Lure?"

Ella sorted through the remaining books in her cardboard box. "Yes!" she said. "Here's Lure. We'll catch plenty of fish with this one."

Soon, there were no books left in the box. And nothing left to pack, except food from the kitchen.

Ella swallowed hard. "I think we're ready," she said.

But her gut twisted, as if to say, *Are you sure?*

* * *

"The golem!" Rowan whispered suddenly. "I forgot about the golem!"

The girls were crouched beside the front steps, loaded down with supplies, armor, and weapons. After days of planning, they had managed to sneak out of the house in the dead of night, only to get no farther than the front gate.

For half a second, Ella felt relief. *So we can't go after all,* she thought. *We'll have to stay.*

But under the weight of her canvas sack, she felt something else—the weight of worry. Ever since she and Rowan had finalized their plans, the howling had gotten more intense. It was as if her wolf knew she was coming and was urging her to hurry—before it was too late.

She stood up slightly to ease the cramping in her legs, and risked a glance through the gate. Sure enough, the iron golem stood watch, shards of light reflecting off his iron body.

"Can we distract him?" she whispered.

Rowan shrugged. "Maybe." She reached for a stone in the gravel and tossed it over the gate.

As the stone *plinked* off a tree branch, the golem startled. He slid sideways toward the orchard, his arms raised and ready for battle.

"Now!" whispered Rowan. She was already running, crouched low, toward the gate.

Ella tried to follow, but another cramp shot through her calf. She shook her leg and hobbled after Rowan. *Please don't let him see us,* she prayed as she ran. *Please, please, please.*

The iron golem stood beneath an apple tree now, shaking the branches. So the girls inched through the cracked gate and ran.

As Ella raced down the steep hill toward the village, her legs nearly gave way. Her armor felt awkward and heavy, and her iron sword clanked at her side.

As she stumbled, she imagined herself rolling, bouncing along like a snowball in the Taiga—the kind that start small and then grow into massive avalanches.

That's how fear began in her chest too, like a small spinning orb that gathered strength with every step.

She was outside the mansion walls now, running away from the safety of the bright courtyard and into the danger of darkness. At any moment, skeletons might spawn, sending arrows whizzing past her ears.

From beneath her leather helmet, she listened for the moan of zombies and the hiss of creepers. Instead, she heard the tinkling of glass bottles—potion bottles? She scanned the hillside for a purple-robed witch ready to launch a potion of harming.

But there was nothing there.

Get a grip! Ella scolded herself. *Be brave—for your wolf. And for Mom. This is your chance to make her proud.*

She pictured her mother's dark hair and flashing eyes, a memory that was eroding along the edges like sandstone. Then she saw something else—Gran's pained face, the way she'd look when she read the letter the girls had left on the kitchen table.

Gran can't protect us anymore, Ella suddenly realized. *And if anything happens to us, well . . . it'll break her heart for good.*

"Hurry up!"

Rowan's voice shot through the darkness like an arrow, and it hit its mark.

Ella shook off her worry and her fear, and just ran.

* * *

"Are we . . . there?" asked Ella, trying to catch her breath. Her legs felt *so* heavy.

When Rowan nodded and pointed toward a shadowy structure up ahead, Ella sunk to her knees with relief.

"Don't stop!" Rowan scolded. "We can rest inside the barn."

She had chosen the barn just yesterday, when the girls had scaled Gran's wall for the last time. "It's halfway between Gran's house and the village," Rowan had said. "It'll keep us safe till morning." She had sounded so sure.

But as Ella neared the barn, nervous thoughts fluttered through her mind. *Are there critters inside? Or mobs? Will there be enough light to keep them from spawning? Will the farmer find us and throw us out?*

Rowan pressed her eye to a knothole in the barn door. "It looks empty," she whispered. "C'mon."

Sure enough, the barn was empty—though it smelled like hay and animal droppings. Animals had lived there not long ago. *So where are they now?* Ella wondered.

As Rowan lit a torch, Ella lowered her sack onto a hay bale. "Sheep's wool," she murmured, picking up tufts of white from the hay. "It must be a sheep farm."

That thought warmed her from the inside out. Suddenly, the hay-bale bed seemed cozy and warm. Ella laid back and let her eyelids drift shut, picturing herself in her room at the mansion.

Then she heard it—the rattle of the barn door.

Ella sat straight up. Someone was trying to get inside! Someone—or *something*.

Rowan pulled her sword and crept toward the barn door. But Ella couldn't move.

Then she heard a squeal.

Was it a ghast? Gran had taught her about the floating white mobs that shot fireballs. The barn would go up in flames in seconds!

No, she reminded herself. *Ghasts only live in the Nether.*

Then she heard it again—a high-pitched screech. But it wasn't a ghast. It wasn't a mob at all.

"Ella! Rowan! Let me in—quick!"

It was *Jack.*

CHAPTER 5

owan lifted the latch and threw open the barn door. But Jack was nowhere to be found.

Ella lunged forward, searching the darkness. Had a mob already gotten to him? Panic rose in her chest.

Then she saw a backpack resting on the ground. *Jack's* backpack.

"Where are you?" she hollered.

"Here!"

His voice rang out clear as a bell, as if he were standing two feet away. Then the backpack floated off the ground—by *itself.*

When Rowan sprang backward, Jack laughed. The pack shook, and glass bottles *tink-tink-tink*ed together.

"Potion of invisibility," Jack explained, his voice filled with pride. "I followed you, and you didn't even know!"

Ella's fear gave way to relief, and then to anger. "Were you spying on us?" She searched the shadows, waiting for her cousin to reappear.

But he fell silent. And then he began to sniffle.

"I d-didn't want to stay behind!" he stammered. "I was afraid you would never come back."

Like our parents, Ella thought, her heart softening.

"But how did you know where we were going?" Rowan demanded.

"Easy," he said. "You were making all that noise with the anvil in the garden shed. I heard what you were planning to do, and I followed you."

Uh-oh. If Jack had heard, Gran might have too. "Does Gran know where we are?" Ella asked quickly.

A tuft of dark hair shook side to side. Jack's head was beginning to reappear. "I didn't tell," he insisted.

Rowan paced back and forth. "We can't take him with us," she said, voicing the words that Ella was already thinking.

"I'm right here," said Jack. "I can hear you. And I'm going with you."

"But you don't have any armor!" said Ella. "So I can't protect you with enchantments. And you don't have any weapons. You have to go back, Jack."

But she knew he couldn't go by himself—he would be in danger. And if they took the time to walk him back, it would be morning by the time they reached the mansion. Gran would be awake and already searching for them.

"I don't need enchantments," said Jack, his face fully visible now. "I have potions." He shook his sack.

"And besides, if you send me back, I'll tell Gran where you are."

"You little snitch!" said Rowan. She was spitting mad now.

Ella took a deep breath and a step forward, between her two cousins. "I don't like it either," she said to Rowan. "But he's here now. We can't leave him behind. And who knows? His potions might come in handy."

Rowan scoffed, but she was softening, Ella could tell.

"No whining," Rowan finally said to Jack. "I'm not carrying your sack for you—Ella won't either. And you have to keep up."

He nodded, his brown eyes wide. "I will. I promise."

But later, as they settled onto the hay bales to sleep, Ella heard the low howl of her wolf. Was he worried? Was he telling her that bringing Jack was a mistake?

As she stared at the cobwebs in the rafters of the barn, Ella wondered again, *How can we protect my wolf, if I don't even know if we can protect ourselves?*

*   *   *

"Are we almost there?"

Under the weight of his backpack, Jack was already lagging behind. Ella fought the urge to carry it for him. If she didn't do something fast, Rowan might decide to send him back—before they'd even reached the village.

"Too bad we can't drink a little potion of swiftness!" Ella joked. If she could get Jack to think about potions, maybe he'd stop whining.

"Hey, good idea!" said Jack. He dropped to the ground and started rummaging through his pack.

"Stop," said Rowan. "Don't use any potions now. We're going to need them *more* later."

Jack turned to Ella with pleading eyes.

"She's right, Jack," Ella had to admit. "We're just getting started. We'll need your potions later on, when we're tired." *Or when we run into hostile mobs,* she thought to herself.

A few minutes later, when Jack sprang ahead, she wondered if he had snuck a bit of the potion. But at least he was moving, and they were almost to the village now. Ella could see the iron golem, standing protectively near a cluster of small buildings.

Ella quickened her pace. She had only been to the village a few times with Gran, but she remembered every moment of those visits. Going to the butcher shop for meat. To the blacksmith to sharpen tools. And *especially* going to the library for books on enchantments.

She had met lots of villagers, but she'd never spoken to them. Whenever she met a stranger, her voice flew away like one of the cave bats Gran had taught her about. She let Gran do the talking.

But not Rowan, thought Ella. *She always speaks for herself.*

So when they reached the edge of the village, Ella wasn't surprised to see Rowan march up to a farmer who was pushing a wheelbarrow toward the market.

"Do you know where I can find a map?" she asked in a clear, bold voice.

The farmer eyed her armor and her sword, and then glanced at Jack and Ella. Ella avoided his gaze and studied the potatoes in his wheelbarrow, as if they were the most interesting things in the world.

"You kids in trouble?" asked the farmer. "Do you need help?"

"No, thanks," said Rowan quickly. "We're fine. We're just in the market for a map."

The farmer stroked his scruffy chin. "Check the library," he said, gesturing toward a building with a long set of stairs. He reached for the handles of his wheelbarrow, but then stopped.

"If you're traveling north, be careful." His brow furrowed with concern. "A pack of wolves has been destroying everything in their path. Chickens, sheep—you name it. Wouldn't be surprised if those vicious creatures attacked children, too."

"Wolves?" said Jack. "That's funny because—"

Ella silenced him with a look.

Jack could be chatty—way *too* chatty sometimes. And she didn't want him telling anyone about her wolf, especially a farmer who thought wolves were "vicious creatures."

Then she remembered the tufts of wool in the barn. Had wolves attacked those sheep?

She'd heard about wolves killing other animals for food. *But they'd never attack kids,* thought Ella, looking the farmer straight in the eye. *At least not* my *wolf.*

She brushed past the farmer and followed her cousins toward the library. But as Rowan took the steps two by two, Ella lagged behind. A librarian was selling books at a table out front, and these weren't ordinary books. No, the lavender glow gave them away. Would there be an enchanted book on the table that Ella hadn't gotten before?

"I'll wait out here!" she called to her cousins. Then she rubbed her hands together as if she'd just discovered a stash of emeralds.

Ella studied the books, one by one. Potion of Efficiency. Silk Touch. Fortune. Those would all be great if she were heading into the mines. But they wouldn't be much help in the forest or the Taiga.

Then a leather-bound book caught Ella's eye. *Frost Walker.* That was definitely an enchantment she'd never gotten, and one she'd never needed—until now. Frost Walker would let her walk across water, turning every drop into ice. *Perfect for the Taiga,* she realized.

As other villagers approached the table, Ella quickly grabbed the book.

"Would you like that one, dear?" asked the librarian.

Ella searched for her voice. "Yes, please," she said. "But . . . do you know where I could find an anvil?" She had to repeat the question twice before the librarian understood.

"Yes, dear. Right over there—at the toolsmith's shop." The librarian gestured to a building two doors down. Then she held out her palm. "That'll be seven emeralds, please."

Uh-oh. The emeralds were all in Rowan's sack. Ella had to wait an embarrassingly long time before Rowan and Jack finally came out of the library. And Rowan didn't seem all too happy about using precious emeralds for a book.

Ella shrugged. How could she explain? The enchanted book had called to her as clearly as her own wolf had, reaching out to her from the Taiga. She could hardly wait to get into the toolsmith's shop to enchant her book!

The librarian patted Ella's hand. "I understand, dear. Enchanted books are treasures, aren't they?" Then she turned to Jack. "I have a boy about your age. Do you kids live nearby?"

Jack shook his head. "We live with Gran in the mansion on the hill." He pointed.

Ella could just make out the beacon rising above the obsidian walls of Gran's mansion. A pang of homesickness pricked her heart. Gran would have found the note by now. She would be worried sick.

One of the villagers turned to look too, and something flickered across her face. Recognition? Did she know Gran?

The woman leaned over and said something to the librarian. It was no more than a whisper, but Ella caught every word.

It's them, she said. *These are the children who live with the witch!*

CHAPTER 6

"**A** witch?" snapped Rowan. "Why would she *say* that?" She turned on her heel, as if she were going to march right back to the table of books and confront the villager.

"Shh!" said Ella. "Keep your voice down." She had waited until they'd left the toolsmith's shop to tell her cousins what she'd heard. *But I should have waited longer,* she realized. *Until we'd left the village.*

"Gran's not a witch!" whispered Jack. "I mean, she brews potions, but . . ."

"So do you," snapped Rowan. "And that doesn't make you a witch, does it? Lots of people brew potions."

Jack's face fell.

"Don't worry about it," said Ella. "Maybe I misunderstood."

She *hoped* she had heard wrong. But there was no

mistaking the look on the villager's face. She seemed to know who Gran was.

And she seemed to know who we are, too, Ella realized. A chill ran down her spine.

* * *

By noon, Ella and her cousins had reached the edge of the woods, where the plains gave way to white birch and oak trees thick with leaves. A worn path led straight into the heart of the forest, winding around a shallow pond.

Rowan tapped the map with her finger. "This is our trail," she said. "It'll lead us to the base of the mountain—the start of the extreme hills."

Ella glanced upward, and then farther up still. She couldn't see the top of the mountain. The sun stung her eyes and made them water. But the view was beautiful.

Slow down to appreciate one beautiful thing every day, Gran always said. So Ella did, just for a moment— until homesickness overwhelmed her, and she had to turn away.

"Can we eat now?" asked Jack, settling down onto a moss-covered stone.

"Yes," said Rowan. "But quickly. We need to get through the forest and build our shelter before nightfall."

Jack unwrapped a sandwich and stared at it, opening and closing the bread as if hoping something delicious would magically appear. "Don't we have anything else?" he asked. "I had one of these for breakfast."

Ella slid something from her sack. "Why don't you fish for our lunch?" she said, handing Jack the fishing pole.

His eyes lit up. He grabbed the pole and searched the perimeter of the pond for the perfect place to cast his line.

"Ella, what are you thinking? We don't have time for fishing," said Rowan.

"Oh, yes we do," said Ella with a grin. "It's an enchanted pole, remember?"

Sure enough, the moment Jack dropped his hook into the water, something tugged at his line.

"I caught one!" he said. He pulled back on the pole and reeled in a wriggling fish.

It wasn't exactly a salmon, but Ella gave him a high-five, just the same. "Let's cook it up," she said.

"Now?" said Rowan. "I told you, we don't have time!"

"And I told you, we *do*," Ella said again, gritting her teeth. Why couldn't Rowan trust her just this once? *I may not be the bravest girl or the best navigator,* she thought. *But I know a thing or two about enchantments.* Before Rowan could protest, Ella used her sword to cook the fish. As soon as the iron tip touched the pink flesh, it began to smoke. Seconds later, they had a crispy, charred little fish, thanks to the Fire Aspect enchantment.

"Cool!" said Jack, tossing his sandwich aside.

Rowan said nothing. She was too busy gobbling up her fish. Then she glanced at Ella, as if hoping for more.

"You're welcome," said Ella. But what she wanted to say was, "Next time, back off. Don't treat me the way you treat Jack."

She followed Rowan in silence as they began their trek through the woods—silence, except for the crackling of twigs and leaves beneath their feet. Sunlight filtered through the trees, sending dappled light onto the trail ahead.

As she walked, Ella tried not to think about Gran. Instead, she listened for the sound of howling. It had been hours now since she'd heard it last. *What does that mean?* she wondered. *Is my wolf okay?*

She walked faster.

Twice, Jack asked if he could use his potion of swiftness to help them get through the forest more quickly. The second time, Rowan chewed her lip, as if considering it. But then she shook her head.

They walked farther, until the sun hung low in the sky and the trees thinned out. The mountains that had seemed so distant from Gran's house were right in front of them now, inviting them upward.

Suddenly, Rowan stopped.

Ella nearly ran into the back of her. "What?" she asked.

Rowan pointed. "I think we just found our shelter for the night. Look!"

Ella stared past a giant oak, toward a pile of lumber. Then she realized it wasn't a pile—it was a weathered old cabin. Built of long planks of wood, the cabin leaned a bit to the right. But it had a roof and a door, which meant it would be safer than sleeping in a pile of brush.

Jack raced toward the front door.

"Wait!" called Rowan. "It might not be empty." She reached for her sword.

Jack slowed to a trot and pressed his face against the cloudy window. He rubbed the grime off and looked again. "I don't see anyone," he said. "But there's a bed. I call dibs on the bed!"

As he reached for the doorknob, Rowan held him back. "Let's light a torch first," she said. "Something could spawn in the shadows."

Ella reached for her torch, too. If there was something inside, would she know how to fight it? Would she be brave enough? Or would she guzzle Jack's potion of swiftness and run away?

Rowan entered the cabin first, very slowly. She held her torch in one hand and her sword in the other. As she disappeared into the shadows, she called over her shoulder, "Coast is clear. C'mon!"

The cabin held a wooden table, two chairs, a furnace, and a bed. Someone had been there recently—Ella could tell by the plate on the table, smeared with breadcrumbs and wet egg yolk.

"Maybe someone lives here," she whispered, checking the room again for signs of life.

Rowan shook her head. "There's no food stored here, or coal. There are only a few chunks left for the furnace. Whoever was here was just passing through."

Ella really hoped she was right.

While Jack unpacked his potions and lined them up on the windowsill, Ella smoothed out the bed covers. Her legs felt so tired after hours of walking. She'd go to bed right now, if she could.

But then I'll only worry about Gran, she decided. *And my wolf.*

She closed her eyes, listening for a howl—or even a whimper. Where had he gone?

It was nearly bedtime when she heard it. Jack had fallen asleep on the floor, wrapped in a wool blanket. Ella had climbed into bed, while Rowan lit a few extra torches to keep mobs away.

That's when the howling started.

Ella sat up and listened.

But it wasn't howling exactly—it was more like barking. And it wasn't just one wolf. It was a whole *pack* of them, their barking and growling getting louder by the second.

They're coming this way! Ella realized.

She locked eyes with Rowan. And for the very first time, she saw fear in her cousin's eyes.

CHAPTER 7

The barking grew louder, as if the wolves were just outside the cabin door. Rowan rushed over to check the latch.

"What's going on?" asked Jack. He rubbed his eyes. When he heard the barking, he jumped to his feet.

Ella stepped in front of him, as if to shield him. *But how can I protect him against a pack of raging wolves?* she wondered. Then she heard something else—the whinny of horses. And a horribly loud *rap* on the cabin door.

Rowan grabbed her sword. "Who is it?" she shouted, her green eyes flashing in the light of the torch.

"We're hunting wolves," said a gruff voice. "A pack of bloodthirsty wolves. Have they come this way?"

Rowan lifted the latch and inched the door open just slightly.

A farmer in brown robes and a scruffy beard stood beside a horse, as if he had just dismounted. Behind him were other men on horseback, holding blazing torches. And on the ground nearby were dozens of wolves—no, *not* wolves. Dogs!

Ella blew out a breath of relief, until she realized what the man had just said. "You're hunting wolves?" she asked.

"Yes," said the farmer. "The nasty beasts are destroying sheep, chicken, pigs—any livestock they can find on farms nearby. It's time to put a stop to it."

Ella didn't hear what Rowan asked him next. Because suddenly, the howling began. It wasn't the dogs outside the cabin that were making the mournful sound. It was Ella's wolf, howling at her to *Hurry! Please hurry!*

Were these men chasing her wolf? Is that what he was running from?

Ella blinked and studied the farmer's face. She had been imagining horrible mobs chasing her wolf and his pack. But maybe it hadn't been mobs at all. Maybe it was *humans,* these villagers who didn't understand wolves. The same villagers who thought her grandmother was a witch.

I'll protect you, she told her wolf. *I'll find a way.*

* * *

"We have to go *now,*" Ella said again. "The wolves are in danger!"

This time, it was Rowan who wasn't ready. "It's not even daylight," she said, checking the window again.

"There are zombies and skeletons roaming the mountainside. Do you want to get us all killed?"

Jack's wide eyes darted from Ella's face to Rowan's and back again. "We can use my potion of night vision," he said sweetly.

That did it. Ella deflated like a pufferfish that had just lost its puff. "Thank you, Jack," she said. "But no. You should save that. We'll wait till morning."

But the wait was excruciating. Ella wished she could use Jack's potion of swiftness on the day-night cycle, to speed up the night and even slow down the day. Because there was still so much ground to cover —a mountainside to scale before she could reach her wolf in the Taiga, where she knew he was waiting for her.

When a shaft of sunlight hit the edge of the table, Ella shot up. "Let's go," she said.

As she led her cousins out of the cabin, she caught a whiff of smoke. Something had been burning. But what? She flashed back to the torches that the farmers had carried. Had they found the wolves?

She jogged toward the trail.

"Be careful," warned Rowan. "There could still be creepers out here, left over from last night."

Who's the scaredy-cat now? Ella wanted to shout over her shoulder.

But when she turned, she caught sight of Jack's face. He looked so young in the morning light, and he wasn't wearing a shred of armor. So she slowed her pace, just a little.

I have to save my wolf. But I have to protect Jack too, she reminded herself. It's what Gran had taught her to do.

* * *

"I can't do it," Jack whined.

They'd been hiking up the mountain for hours now. Ella wanted to whine, too. She wanted to lie down and curl up in a ball on the trail. But the frigid mountain air kept her moving forward. They were nearing the Taiga now—she could feel it.

Clouds had rolled in, blocking the warmth of the sun. And then the first raindrop fell, stinging Ella's cheek.

"Rain!" said Jack, sticking out his tongue to catch the droplets.

Rowan scowled. "Rain means no sunlight. No light means *mobs* spawning."

"Huh?" said Jack. "They only come out at night!"

"Not true," said Rowan. She spun in a slow circle, scanning the mountainside. "Mobs spawn at night, *and* in low light."

Ella shivered. "So we need to find shelter," she said, trying to hold her voice steady.

But a quick search revealed nothing—no cabins magically appeared the way one had in the forest. And the sky was growing darker.

"Look for a cave opening," urged Rowan. "Help us, Jack!"

Ella nudged him along the trail. "It'll be like a treasure hunt," she said. "Maybe we'll find a cave with emeralds." *Or maybe we'll find a cave filled with bats!* said the pesky voice in her head.

The rain was really pouring down now. It bounced off Ella's helmet and chestplate, and ran in rivers down her leggings—straight into her enchanted boots, where it turned to ice. *Brrr.*

"There!"

It was Jack who found the cave. The opening was little more than a hole where a boulder had rolled away. But when Rowan lit a torch just inside the opening, Ella saw that the cavern extended deep into the mountainside.

"Do you think there are bats in there?" she whispered.

Rowan shrugged. "Maybe. They're harmless though. C'mon." She ducked and led the way into the cave, with Jack close behind.

Ella paused outside, just long enough to imagine those cave bats, swooping at her through the shadows.

Just long enough to hear a low moan rise up from behind her. Just long enough to whirl around—and come face to face with a zombie.

CHAPTER 8

Time slowed down as the zombie stepped forward, his groan turning into a growl. Folds of rotten flesh hung from his face, and his putrid stench sent a wave of nausea through Ella's stomach.

Run, said a quiet voice in her head. And then louder, *Run!* But her limbs were frozen to the earth.

Then a sword flashed through the darkness like lightning. The zombie grunted and fell backward. And Rowan tugged on Ella's arm, dragging her into the cave.

Before Ella could speak, Rowan had hoisted a large stone in front of the opening to block it. Then she whirled around. "Are you okay?" she asked. "Did it hurt you?"

Ella shook her head. "No. I don't know. I don't think so." Then her knees buckled and she plunked to the cold ground, shaking.

"It's okay," said Jack, patting her shoulder the way Gran might. But Ella could feel him trembling too.

Get it together, she ordered herself. *Be brave for Jack.*

"I'm alright," she told him. "That zombie didn't stand a chance. Not with Rowan and her enchanted sword here to protect us."

She shot Rowan a grateful smile, but Rowan was pacing. She strode the length of the cave and back again.

"Zombies are the slowest mobs," she said. "You don't have to fight them, Ella, but you have to at least outrun them."

Is she scolding me? thought Ella.

"You can't just stand there and let them destroy you. And I won't always be there to save you!"

Rowan's words felt like a punch in the stomach. Ella could barely breathe, let alone respond.

But Jack did. He puffed out his chest. "You don't have to save *me*," he said. "If those zombies show up again, I'll blast them with a splash potion." He shook a glass bottle in his hand.

He probably will, thought Ella bitterly. *Maybe Jack doesn't need me to protect him. He's brave, like Rowan. But me? At the first sign of danger, I freeze up like an icicle.*

The cave filled with silence, except for the *drip-drip-drip* of rainwater seeping through the cracks.

Finally, Rowan sighed and slid down the cave wall until she was sitting beside Ella. "Let's just wait out the storm," she said. "And rest up. Because we still have a long way to go."

Ella dropped her head backward against the wall. *Rest?* She couldn't, because resting meant worry— worry about Gran and worry about her wolf. But this time, as Ella closed her eyes, it wasn't Gran's face she saw. And it wasn't her wolf, with his anguished eyes.

No, when Ella closed her eyes now, all she could see was that moaning mob, staggering toward her, step by horrifying step.

* * *

"Help me move the rock," said Rowan, shaking Ella awake.

The rain had stopped, and pricks of sunlight shone through cracks in the wall. *Finally,* thought Ella.

She pushed against the rock with all her weight, and felt it give beneath her.

"Wait!" said Rowan. "Let me check for mobs." She stuck her head outside—and suddenly started laughing.

"What?" asked Ella. What could possibly be so funny?

"Carrots!" said Rowan. "The zombie dropped car- rots. Oh, and a potato. Just in time for lunch."

"I like carrots," said Jack, yawning.

When Rowan offered Ella a carrot, she shook her head. The thought of eating something that had dropped from that disgusting mob made her stom- ach turn over. And anyway, her wolf was back now. He wasn't howling exactly. He was whining. Fretting. Pacing. Waiting. She felt his worry, sending waves of restlessness through her own body.

"Can we get going?" she asked. "The storm has passed, and we've wasted enough time."

Rowan checked the sky again. "There are more dark clouds rolling in. We're going to have to move quickly—and keep our eyes open for shelter along the way."

Jack shook his backpack, reminding the girls of the bottles inside. "Potion of swiftness?" he asked hopefully.

"No," said Rowan. "Not yet."

But Ella's frustration spilled over. "What are we waiting for?" she asked. "You told us we have to move quickly—that another storm is coming. And my wolf is in danger. So what are we saving the potion for?"

Rowan raised a single eyebrow, then released a long, slow breath. "Fine," she said. "Have it your way. But don't come crying to me when we're being chased by a pack of zombie pigmen, and we're all out of potion of swiftness."

Yes! For the first time in days, Ella felt hopeful. With Jack's potions, maybe they *would* get to her wolf in time. *Hang on,* she told him. *We're coming.*

"Zombie pigmen?" Jack scrunched up his forehead. "They live in the Nether, not the Taiga."

"Very good," said Ella. "Gran taught you well. But did you hear what Rowan said? Bust out that potion, Jack!"

As he poured out the contents of his backpack, Ella winced, hoping none of the bottles would shatter on the cave floor. He sorted them by color—from red and orange to pink, purple, and blue. Then he grabbed the lavender-blue bottle and untwisted the cap.

"Who wants to go first?" he asked.

"Wait till we're all packed up and ready to go," said Rowan. "So the potion doesn't wear off too quickly."

"It won't!" said Jack, suddenly sounding very grown-up. "I added Redstone."

Rowan's eyebrow shot up again, and she glanced at Ella. "Do we trust his brewing skills?" she asked. "If I drink this, will I grow another head? Or turn into a scuttlefish?"

Jack laughed out loud. "No!"

Ella cracked a smile, too. "Give it to me, Jack—I'll go first." She took a quick swig, expecting the potion to taste bitter or slimy. But it didn't. It tasted like . . . sugar. "Yum. I forgot you made this with sugar from Gran's sugar cane!" Her words tumbled out so quickly, she slapped her hand over her mouth.

Jack grinned. "See? The potion's working already."

Seconds later, Ella wasn't only talking fast—she was *walking* fast. It was as if her legs were racing each other, the left against the right. She felt as if she were *leaping* up the mountain. Her canvas sack felt light as a feather, and as the trail grew steeper, her legs only grew stronger.

Rowan was still in the lead, but just barely. Even the usually poky Jack flew up the trail, grinning from ear to ear.

As they crested the top of a rocky hill, Ella heard the bubbling of water. A narrow mountain stream wound its way near the trail, close enough for Jack to leap across, back and forth.

Ella would have scolded him for wasting time, except that he *wasn't* wasting time—he flew across that stream fast as a bird and nimble as the sheep roaming the rocky hillside.

She even took a second to dip her own toe into the stream. Instantly, the water beneath her boot turned to ice. She jumped back in surprise. "Oh, hey! Enchanted boots!"

The Frost Walker worked like a charm, just like Jack's potion. Quick as lightning, Ella walked across the stream, feeling ice form beneath each step. By the time she'd reached the other side, it had melted again, and the stream bubbled onward.

When a gentle rain began to fall, Ella felt invincible—as if she could dodge the droplets. She darted around them, between them, and beneath them.

"Isn't it fun?" Jack called to Ella, his high-pitched voice sounding like a music disc that had been sped up or fast-forwarded.

She laughed. "Yes! Very fun. Why didn't we drink this potion sooner?"

Rowan shot her a glare, but Ella ignored her. Even as the sky darkened, she felt joyful. *I can outrun any storm,* she told herself.

But ahead on the damp trail, Rowan stopped suddenly and whirled around.

Ella skidded to a stop, too. Her body trembled, eager to race on ahead. "What? What's wrong?" She couldn't hide the irritation in her voice. Why did Rowan keep slowing them down?

Rowan crouched low and pointed down into the valley. She waved Ella to the rocky edge.

Ella grabbed a thin tree trunk to steady herself and then leaned lower. But before she could see anything, something whizzed past her ear and pierced the tree.

It quivered there in the wood, just beside her head.

An *arrow*.

CHAPTER 9

"**S**keletons!" shouted Rowan. She grabbed her bow and arrow in a flash.

Ella's mind raced. *Get down. Get your bow. Protect Jack.*

"Get down, Jack!" she hollered. "Hide!"

Then she reached for her own bow, the one she'd practiced with just once before leaving Gran's house. She placed an arrow in the bow the way Rowan had shown her, and pulled back the bowstring. Then she willed herself to look over the edge of the rock.

The skeletons were climbing quickly. She had just enough time to count them—one, two, three—before another arrow flew overhead.

Rowan shouted something Ella couldn't hear over the rushing sound in her ears. *Don't panic!* she told herself. *Be brave!*

She released her arrow . . . and missed the skeleton by a mile. Her arrow disappeared into the cloudy sky.

Try again. You can do this.

Thwang! Thunk! Her next arrow flew straight into the earth.

You're wasting arrows! she scolded herself—until she remembered that she'd given her bow the Infinity enchantment. She would never run out of arrows. *But what good is that if my arrows never hit their mark?*

The skeletons were close enough now to see their gaping eyes and mouths, and to hear their bones rattling. Ella's arms shook as she released another arrow.

Thwack!

The skeleton grunted and buckled. As he hit the ground, he burst into flames.

"I got him!" Ella shouted.

"No, I got him," said Rowan as she shifted her aim to the other skeletons. *Thwang! Thwack!*

The second skeleton exploded into flames.

Right, thought Ella, sinking to the ground. She'd given Rowan's bow the Flame enchantment. So it was Rowan's arrow that had taken out the skeleton, not her own.

As Rowan reached for another arrow, Ella watched the third skeleton, waiting for him to meet his fiery death.

Crack! Splash!

Glass shattered, and the skeleton fell backward in a haze of maroon bubbles.

"Got him!" shouted Jack, punching his fist.

But as Ella watched with horror, the skeleton lunged forward again.

Thwack! Thwack, thwack! He released a barrage of arrows.

"Get down, Jack!" cried Ella, leaping backward to shield him. She landed on him hard and held on tight.

"Get off!" he cried.

But she wouldn't. Not till she heard the grunt of the skeleton and the crackling of flames. *Rowan got him,* she thought with relief. *It's over.*

As Ella rolled off Jack, he swatted her with his hands. "Why'd you do that?" he cried. "I was going to throw another splash potion!"

Ella grabbed his hands to stop him. "I was *protecting* you!" she cried. "You don't have a helmet on, Jack."

"I don't need one!" he cried. "I have my potions!" He grabbed his backpack as if to show her. But as he lifted it off the ground, something dripped out the bottom.

Rainwater? wondered Ella.

No—the liquid shimmered with color as it swirled into a bubbly pool on the rocks below.

"Look what you did!" cried Jack.

Ella knew in an instant. *I broke his bottles,* she realized. *I was trying to protect him, and I destroyed his precious potions!*

"I'm sorry, Jack," she said quickly. "There's still some left, see?" She carefully emptied the damp backpack, showing him the bottles that remained. But shards of glass littered the ground around them.

"Don't touch anything," warned Rowan. "Let the rain wash off the potions first."

I won't touch anything, thought Ella bitterly. *I've already done enough damage.*

Jack wouldn't even look at her.

And the rain just kept coming.

* * *

"I wish you two would stop moping already," said Rowan. "We fought off the skeletons. You should be happy!"

You and Jack fought off the skeletons, Ella wanted to say. *I didn't fight a single thing, except a few glass bottles.*

Jack looked like he would never be happy again, even though his backpack was probably a whole lot lighter now.

"We even picked up some bones and arrows the skeletons had dropped," said Rowan. "Get it? Bones and arrows?"

She wiggled her eyebrows in Ella's face. "You know, bones and arrows instead of bows and arrows?"

"Not funny," said Ella. Who could joke at a time like this? But she *was* glad for the skeleton bone. She reached into her cape pocket to make sure it was still there. *I'll feed that to my wolf. That is, if I ever find him,* she thought miserably.

Her feet felt cold and heavy, like ice blocks. She could see the snowcapped mountains ahead. They would reach the Taiga by tomorrow night, Rowan had said. But that meant another long day of walking, and more battles to fight.

Jack dragged his feet, too.

"Hurry up!" Rowan called over her shoulder.

But Ella couldn't hurry, no matter how hard she tried. The potion of swiftness had worn off and taken her energy—and her hope—along with it.

After another hour of trudging along the trail, Rowan pointed to something in the distance. Animals grazed on a rocky hillside speckled with wild grass.

Ella strained to see. "Are those sheep?" she asked.

"No!" scoffed Rowan. *"Horses."* She didn't just say the word. She breathed it in, as if the word itself had magical powers.

"Yeah, so?" said Ella. She didn't mean to sound grumpy, but what was the big deal?

Rowan cocked her head. "I think they're *wild* horses."

For some reason Ella didn't understand, Rowan had a thing for wild horses. They'd never actually seen a wild horse—only the thick, muscular horses farmers used to plow fields.

And to hunt wolves, Ella remembered with a shiver.

"Let's go look!" said Rowan. She scampered up the trail, as if Jack had given her another swig of potion of swiftness.

"Wait up!" cried Jack from down below.

"Don't bother, Jack," grumbled Ella. "She spotted wild horses. There's no stopping her now."

But as they neared the rocky hillside, Rowan hung

her head. "They're not wild," she said. "There's a fence. See?"

Ella followed the fence with her eyes all the way to a farmhouse and a cluster of outbuildings. Remembering the soft hay bales they had slept on the very first night, she grabbed Rowan's hand. "Can we stay in one of those barns tonight?" she asked.

"Yes, please," said Jack. "I'm tired."

Ella expected Rowan to say no. They hadn't gotten very far today because of the storm—and the skeletons.

But Rowan gazed again at the horses and actually said, "Yes."

Ella nearly dropped her canvas sack with surprise.

"But let's be careful," Rowan warned. "We'll have to hide from the farmers until dusk."

They waited just past the fence, ducking down in the grass and eating a few mushy apples for dinner.

"I wish there was a fishing pond," said Jack.

Ella's mouth watered, too, at the thought of charred fish. But she didn't say so. She didn't want to be a whiner, not after Rowan had let them stop early for the night.

When dusk finally fell, Rowan led them along the fence toward the oldest-looking barn—the one farthest from the house.

There were plenty of knotholes in the wood for them to peek through. All three cousins lined up, searching the shadows of the barn for any signs of life. Through her peephole, Ella saw nothing but a rusty hoe hanging on a hook.

"Looks like a tool shed," said Rowan. "Coast is clear."

She slid open the barn door, careful not to make a sound.

As Ella stepped inside, she smelled must and dust—not the sweet smell of fresh hay. *Drat.* But as night fell, weariness set in. Her body felt so *heavy*, even after she stripped out of her armor and lay down on a dusty blanket.

The last thing she heard was the whinny of a horse.

She dreamed of Rowan, walking through the field and offering an apple to a chestnut-colored horse.

But it wasn't Rowan walking. It's *me*, Ella realized. She could feel the apple in her palm.

Then it wasn't a horse at all. It was her wolf. He licked her hand and pressed his trembling body against her legs. Then he raised his muzzle toward the moon and let out a gut-wrenching howl.

He's so sad! she realized.

She dropped down beside him and stroked his thick, wiry fur. *Tell me what's wrong*, she said. *Tell me what I can do.*

But he didn't tell her. He *showed* her.

The wolf led the way through the field, turning to make sure she followed. He led her toward the horses that were grazing. But they weren't horses either— they were wolves. They were all lying down, sleeping soundly.

As Ella bent to stroke one of the wolves, its body felt cold and rigid beneath her touch.

And that's when she knew.

The wolves aren't sleeping, she realized with horror. *They're dying.*

CHAPTER 10

"I'm going!" Ella cried. "You can't stop me." She reached again for the latch on the barn door.

"Not in the middle of the night!" said Rowan. "We've already been through this." She flung her body against the door, blocking Ella's path.

Rage burned hot in Ella's chest. She leaned forward until she was inches away from Rowan's face. "The wolves are *dying*," she said through gritted teeth. "I'm *going*."

The next few seconds passed like hours.

Ella saw the shift in Rowan's expression. She licked her lips. "Then we're going too," Rowan finally said. "Just wait for us. Please?"

Ella blinked into the darkness. Was Rowan actually listening to her?

Rowan quickly packed her sack and rustled Jack from sleep. "Keep your weapons drawn. This is going to be a long night," she said to Ella. "I don't know how we're going to make it through." She added the last part under her breath, as if talking to herself.

Then, as if in response, a horse whinnied from the pasture.

Rowan whirled around and cocked her head, listening.

"It's just a horse," said Ella. Was Rowan going to be spooked by every little noise?

Rowan shushed her. When the horse whinnied again, her eyes flashed with excitement.

"What?" said Jack. "What did it say to you?"

"She's offering help," Rowan whispered. "A way to get to the Taiga safely."

Ella caught Rowan's eye. *For real?* she asked with a single glance. She had heard a whinny. But somehow, her cousin had heard so much more.

Rowan nodded solemnly. And smiled.

*   *   *

"Just hang on," Rowan said.

Ella didn't need to be told twice. She was wedged in the saddle between Rowan and Jack. *So who do I hold on to?* she wondered, suddenly picturing Jack spilling off the back of the chestnut mare. She reached one arm around Rowan's middle, and the other one backward to grab Jack's leg.

Rowan clucked her tongue, and the horse broke into a trot, sending Ella slipping sideways. She scrambled to right herself.

Rowan tapped her heels against the horse's sides, and the horse sped up. Its stride lengthened into a smooth gallop.

Ella marveled at its speed—and at Rowan's skills. "When did you learn how to ride a horse?" she hollered into the wind.

Rowan glanced over her shoulder. "I didn't!" she said.

Yet somehow, she just knew. *Maybe her horse is telling her,* Ella realized. *Rowan talks with horses the way I talk with my wolf.*

But her wolf had fallen silent again.

She pictured the wolves' bodies littering the pasture, and dread crept from her head to her toes. She tapped her heels against the horse ever so slightly, and held on tight as the mare quickened her pace.

Suddenly, the horse skidded sideways and whinnied.

"Hold on!" cried Rowan as the saddle shifted beneath them.

Then the horse took off like a shot, as if she'd been struck by an arrow from behind.

Ella whirled around to see what had spooked her. She caught sight of a green, hissing creeper moments before it exploded, uprooting a bush and sending rocks flying.

"Creepers!" she cried. "Mobs are spawning."

"Of course they are," said Rowan. "I told you they would. But our horse knows she can outrun them, don't you, girl?"

She reached down to pat the horse's neck.

The mare blew a puff of steamy air from her nostrils, as if to say, *Don't worry. I won't let you down.*

Relief washed over Ella. She felt safer now, wedged between her cousins on the back of a galloping horse.

It's going to be okay, she told herself. *We'll get there in time.*

They sped through the hills until the rain turned to snow, and a white blanket covered the ground below. Trees sprouted left and right—spruces decorated with white icing.

The Taiga! thought Ella with excitement. *This is my one beautiful thing today, Gran. But I can't slow down to enjoy it—there's no time.*

The horse galloped around a frozen pond and alongside a rushing river. Chunks of ice floated downstream, dodging rocks in small waterfalls.

Ella shivered and leaned into Rowan for warmth. Behind her, Jack snuggled close too, squeezing her middle.

"Are w-we almost th-there?" he asked, his teeth chattering.

"We *are* there," Ella said. "It'll warm up though—the sun is coming up."

The orange globe was just peeking over the horizon. The first few rays felt heavenly as Ella lifted her face to the sun.

"We aren't there *yet*," corrected Rowan. "I mean, we've reached the Taiga. But my map can't help us anymore. You're going to have to lead us from here on out."

Who's she talking to? wondered Ella. *Her horse?*

Rowan spun in the saddle to face Ella. "*You* have to lead us to your wolf," she said solemnly.

Ella caught her breath. "But . . . I don't know where he is. He's so quiet now."

"So listen harder," said Rowan gently.

Ella squeezed her eyes shut. *I'm here!* she called to him. *I'm in the Taiga. But where are you? Show me the way!*

The wind whistled in her ears, and snow swirled around her. Her feet felt frozen solid, as if packed in ice. And she was so *hungry.* A delicious smell wafted from a snow house up ahead. As she padded toward it, she felt the fur on her neck stand on end. There was food here, but also danger. She whined and paced the perimeter of the house, wishing the others were here. But they were gone. Her family—her pack—was gone.

Ella's eyes flew open. "I . . . I saw him," she whimpered. "I *was* him. He's so hungry! And he's all alone. There's food in the snow house, but it's dangerous too. Oh, poor boy!"

"The snow house?" asked Rowan. "Do you mean an igloo?"

Ella hesitated. Gran had taught them about the igloos in the Cold Taiga, built from nothing but blocks of snow. "Yes," she said slowly. "I think that's it. He's in the Cold Taiga!"

Rowan nodded. "We have a bit farther to go." She whispered something in the mare's ear, and the horse lunged forward.

Rowan patted her side. "That's a good girl. When we get there, we'll give you some food and rest."

The horse nickered a response that only Rowan understood.

At the mention of food, Ella's stomach clutched. But it wasn't her own hunger twisting her insides. It was her wolf's. He was starving. And alone. And in danger.

The Cold Taiga was near, but not near enough.

*   *   *

"This isn't an igloo," said Ella. "I told you my wolf was outside an igloo!"

Rowan sighed. "And I told you that we'd traveled far enough. Our horse needs to rest, and so do we. This shelter will have to do."

Shelter? Ella glanced around the small room. It was more like a cave built into the base of a hill, but she had to admit that it was much warmer in here than it was outside.

"Can't we bring the horse in?" asked Jack. "She's cold out there."

"She'll be alright," said Rowan. "I wiped her down and put a blanket on her."

Ella had noticed that it wasn't a blanket, though—it was Rowan's own cape. She had lovingly draped the black wool over her horse's back, even though that left her own arms bare and cold. *She loves her horse as much as I love my wolf,* Ella realized.

While the horse rested, Ella tried to be patient. She helped Rowan light a fire, and they melted snow for the horse in a bucket they'd found in the shelter. They gave her the last of the mushy apples, too, which she chomped down greedily.

Then the girls joined Jack inside, where he picked at a sandwich and took stock of his potions.

When the horse nickered, Rowan stood and brushed off her leggings. "She's ready," she said.

"Give me your things and I'll pack her saddle bags."

Rowan took the canvas sacks and Jack's backpack, and stepped outside to strap them onto her horse's saddle.

"Did you get enough to eat?" Ella asked Jack.

He shrugged. "Are there places to fish in the Cold Taiga?" he asked.

Ella nodded. "Probably. We might have to break a hole in the ice first," she said, reaching over to smooth the cowlick in his hair.

That's when she heard a growl from just outside the shelter.

And a whinny.

And a scream.

Rowan.

CHAPTER 11

"Stay inside!" Ella ordered.

Jack backed away obediently as she pushed past him. She grabbed her sword, feeling it slip in her sweaty palm. Then she stepped outside.

Rowan was tearing up the hillside through the snow, as if something were chasing her. But when Ella looked again, she realized that Rowan was the one doing the chasing. But what was running away from her? Her horse?

No. As Ella's eyes adjusted to the brightness, she saw an enormous snow monster lumbering ahead of Rowan.

"A polar bear!" cried Jack.

"Get back inside!" cried Ella, but this time, he wouldn't budge.

The polar bear reared up on its hind legs and let out a *roar* that rumbled across the Taiga, sending chunks of snow and ice sliding down the hillside. Was he going to turn on Rowan?

"Rowan!" cried Ella. "Stop!" She raced toward her cousin, crunching through the snow. But every few feet, she tripped and fell. Her boots were clunky, and the hill was so steep. "Rowan!"

Ella pushed herself up and reached for her bow. *I might miss the bear,* she realized, *but maybe I can scare it.*

She released an arrow upward, and then watched in horror as it whizzed toward Rowan. It missed her—but only barely.

Rowan whirled around in shock, and finally stopped running.

As she began walking back, Ella sunk to her knees with relief. "Hurry!" she called to Rowan. What if the bear turned around and came after her?

She shaded her eyes and searched for him, but he had disappeared along the snowy horizon. *Thank goodness.*

When Rowan was a few feet away, Ella saw tears frozen to her cheeks. "What is it?" she asked.

"Our horse ran away," said Rowan, struggling to catch her breath. "She was spooked by the bear."

"It's okay," Ella said quickly. "She'll be back."

Rowan shook her head. "No, she's heading home— I'm sure of it. And . . . she's taking our *bags* with her." Her voice broke.

"She'll come back!" Ella insisted. "She's *your* horse now."

Rowan released a heavy sigh. "No, she's not," she said. "It's not like with your wolf, Ella. That horse already has a home—I knew that when I found her. And she needed to go back to stay safe. I just wish she hadn't taken our bags and backpacks with her!"

"What?" said Jack, his lip trembling. "She took my potions?"

His question hung frozen in the air.

"Your potions?" said Rowan. An edge crept into her voice. "You're worried about your *potions*? What about our food? And how are we going to light torches and fire without our flint and steel? Or make it home without my map? How are we going to get to the igloo by the river if we have to pass a pack of polar bears on foot? Did you think about any of that?"

Jack took a step backward.

"Shh," said Ella, "you're scaring him."

"He should be scared," said Rowan bitterly.

"We still have our weapons and our armor," Ella pointed out. "We still have . . ."

Something Rowan had said made her pause.

"Wait, did you say you saw an igloo by a river?"

Rowan wiped her face and nodded. "I saw it when I reached the top of the hill. It's just over the other side, by the river—near the falls."

Ella tingled from her head to her toes. Maybe this was *her* igloo, where she would find her wolf. "We've got to go," she said. "Now!"

Rowan grabbed her by the arm. "Stop. The igloo isn't the only thing I saw over the hill. There are more polar bears—two or three of them. So we're not going now. We'll wait till morning."

Wait? Ella yanked her arm free. She was done waiting. *My wolf could be just over that ridge. What if the polar bears get to him before I do?*

"I'm going to find the igloo," she said, her voice frigid as the icicles hanging from the rim of the water bucket. "You don't get to decide what I do."

"Yes, I do," spat Rowan, her eyes ablaze. "You know why? Because Gran put me in charge. My whole life, she's told me that I have to look out for you. So that's what I'm doing, whether you like it or not."

Rowan spun around and pushed her way into the shelter. Jack followed on her heels, as if he'd already accepted that she was the leader.

But Ella stayed behind. She replayed Rowan's words over and over. *Gran put her in charge,* she thought. *So even Gran thinks I can't take care of myself.*

Finally, when she could no longer feel her fingertips, Ella reached for the door. But by then, she'd made up her mind.

She was going to prove to Gran—and to Rowan— that she could look after herself *and* her wolf. She was going to find the igloo, and she was going to do it tonight. All on her own.

* * *

As Ella pushed open the door, it let out the faintest *squeak*. She glanced back at her cousins. Jack was sleeping soundly, snoring like a baby bear. But what about Rowan? Ella couldn't tell. She hovered for a moment, listening, and then stepped into the frozen night.

As she trudged up the hill into darkness, she raised her torch high, feeling a twinge of guilt for taking it from the shelter. But Rowan and Jack still had a fire to keep them safe and warm. And Rowan had stockpiled enough wood to keep it burning for at least another day.

But when it burns out, then what? asked a tiny voice in Ella's head. *Without flint and steel, how will you ever light another fire—or another torch?*

She blew that worry out with her frozen breath. Then she set her sights on the crest of the hill. She could *feel* her wolf now. He wasn't howling anymore—he didn't have to. He was so close, he could reach out to her with just a whimper.

Tell me where you are, she told him. *Lead me to the igloo.*

She listened, but heard only the *crunch, crunch, crunch* of her boots in the crusty snow.

It was so very dark. Ella glanced up. If the moon was out tonight, it was hiding behind a ceiling of clouds.

Every few steps, she glanced backward to see if she was being followed. She half-expected Rowan to come bursting out of the shelter. She half-*wanted* her to, because she suddenly felt so lonely. *Is this how my wolf feels, too?* she wondered. *Wherever he is?*

To keep her mind busy, Ella began to chant.

Left, right, look forward and back.

Left, right, look forward and back.

The words kept her fear at bay.

Left, right, look forward and—

Ella froze. Something had appeared in the darkness behind her, toward the base of the hill. Two glowing eyes fixed their gaze on her. Two *purple* eyes.

Ella wracked her brain to remember what Gran had taught her about the mobs in the Overworld. What had purple eyes? A witch? A cave spider? The Ender Dragon itself?

Not an Ender Dragon, she suddenly remembered. *An Enderman! Look away! Quick!*

She dropped her gaze to a patch of snow. As the dark, long-legged mob growled, she inched slowly backward. *Don't look up,* she willed herself. If she did, the Enderman might teleport to her side in seconds. Would her armor protect her from harm? Or would she have to fight off the mob with her sword?

Faster and faster, she stepped, until the hill flattened and she lost her footing. She landed hard on her rump and rolled—once, twice, three times. Only then, with the crest of the hill as her shield, did she chance a glance.

The horizon was pitch-black. The glowing eyes were now swallowed up in darkness, just like the stars in the cloud-covered sky.

Relief exploded in Ella's chest, and she took a few ragged breaths. Then she pushed herself to her feet and began to run.

With each downward step, Ella scanned the valley below, searching for her igloo. The shadows played tricks on her. Stones looked like scuttlefish. Gnarly trees stalked her like bony skeletons. And water sprayed off the river rocks like a hissing creeper, about to explode.

What was that hulking shape alongside the river? *My igloo?* Ella wondered. Her heart quickened.

Something moved just beside the igloo—an animal creeping on uncertain legs. *My wolf!* Ella sucked in her breath. Was he weak with hunger?

She raced forward, squinting through the veil of darkness. Any moment now, she'd be by his side. She could wrap her arms around his neck and bury her face in his scruff.

But just as Ella allowed herself to hope, the igloo rose off the ground with a horrific roar.

She knew now that it was *not* an igloo.

It was a polar bear.

CHAPTER 12

Ella stopped so suddenly, she fell to her knees. Her torch sailed out of her hand and landed in the wet snow, sizzling and spitting until the flames turned to smoke.

But there was no time to worry about her torch now.

She sat frozen, torn between running away from the polar bear or running *toward* her wolf. He looked so small, so weak and vulnerable. She pushed herself up and took a step forward.

The bear reared again and roared. Then it lumbered up the hill toward Ella, swinging its enormous head.

Ella hesitated. Could she leave her wolf? Would he be safe? While she watched, the wolf stood on his hind legs to sniff the air. And Ella saw that it wasn't a wolf at all. Her heart sank.

She'd been running toward a polar bear cub—a

tiny bear, with a very protective mother. *Who's coming after me,* Ella realized. *Run!*

She knew instantly that she couldn't outrun the bear. She could only raise her sword and hope that her enchanted armor would protect her.

So Ella whirled around, sword extended, as the bear raged in her direction. Just before it tackled her to the ground, she squeezed her eyes shut. She pictured her mother's face. Then, with a rush of cool air, the bear raced *past* her—and kept going.

Ella wobbled and spun around.

The bear hadn't been charging at her at all! It had set its sights on someone else—*something* else. Ella saw the mobs creeping over the top of the hill, staggering forward with their arms extended.

Zombies? There were so many of them! Two dozen or more. And some carried swords at their sides.

What had Rowan told her about zombies? *You don't have to fight them, but you have to at least outrun them.*

But Ella couldn't run. She couldn't even look away, because something was so strange about these zombies. What was it?

As the bear tackled the first zombie to the ground, the mob squealed with pain or surprise. In an instant, the other zombies rushed to its defense. They weren't moving slowly now at all. They were furiously *sprinting*, swords raised, toward the bear.

And someone was sprinting toward Ella, too. "Run!"

She recognized the voice before she recognized the girl. It was Rowan, her face fierce. She dragged

Jack behind her so quickly, his feet barely touched the ground.

"I said, run!" she hollered again.

So Ella did. She turned and ran for her life, with Rowan and Jack close behind. She could barely feel her legs. Her breath came in short bursts. And then, *thud*—she smacked into a wall of snow.

Rowan tumbled into the wall beside her.

"Are we trapped?" asked Ella. She fought back panic as she patted the wall, searching for a gate or an opening.

The wall curved in a semicircle, and suddenly Ella wasn't touching snow anymore. She felt wet ice beneath her palms. Through the sheet of ice, she heard something. She pressed her ear closer. Music!

It's a window, she realized. *To a house—made of snow and ice.*

"An igloo!" cried Jack.

Yes! They had found her igloo! But squealing, grunting zombies were on their heels now.

"Find the door!" cried Rowan.

Ella circled the wall of snow, desperately searching for the entrance. Suddenly, the wall extended outward, a tunnel that she hoped would lead to safety. "This way!" she called.

As Rowan flew past her into the mouth of the tunnel, Ella reached back for Jack's hand. She heard the *thwack* of a sword hitting a snow block behind her.

"Go!" she hollered to Jack, pushing him ahead of her down the tunnel. He fell forward into darkness.

Then Ella burst through the door behind him, tumbled into the room, and hit the floor.

* * *

"Are the zombies still out there?" asked Jack. Even in the darkness of the igloo, Ella could tell he was trembling.

As if in response, the mobs thumped against the door again. The sound sickened Ella. She prayed the lock on the door would hold. Then she closed her eyes and focused on the music from the jukebox. She could almost imagine Gran humming along.

"I told you, they're not zombies," said Rowan somberly. "They're zombie pigmen."

Ella's eyes sprang open. "Wait, what?" she said. "But zombie pigmen are only found in the Nether!"

"They're *usually* found in the Nether," said Rowan. "But they can come through portals. And when you make one of them angry, well . . . look out." She fumbled in the dark for an overturned chair, set it back upright, and slumped onto it.

"Is that why they were chasing you?" asked Ella. "Did you make one angry?"

Rowan snorted. "Yes, I made one angry. Because I was protecting Jack. Which I wouldn't have had to do if *you* hadn't left in the middle of the night. How could you do that, Ella? How could you put us all in danger?"

Ella shrugged. "My wolf—"

"Forget your wolf!" spat Rowan. "Haven't we lost enough already? Our flint and steel, our food, our map.

And now, thanks to you, I've lost my sword, too. We've lost *everything*."

"What?" said Ella. "What happened to your sword?"

"She dropped it," Jack explained. "And a pigman picked it up."

Ella blew out her breath. So now a zombie pigman was roaming the hillside with Rowan's enchanted sword. *Great.*

"You can use mine," she offered. "With the Fire Aspect enchantment." She pulled it from its sheath.

But as Rowan spun in her seat, she accidentally knocked the sword from Ella's hands. "Don't you see? Your enchantments don't matter!" she said. "We need food and fire more than we need an enchanted sword. It's freezing in here, and if we can't light a torch, we'll have mobs crawling all over us in no time. We won't even make it till morning."

Jack turned to Ella, eyes wide. "Is that true?" he asked.

Ella avoided his gaze, because it *was* true. Rowan was right, as usual. She dropped to the frigid ground and patted around for her sword. Instead, she found a piece of splintered wood—a broken broomstick or chair leg. She crawled farther and found her sword, resting next to the furnace. *So we have wood and a furnace to burn it in, but no flame,* Ella thought miserably.

Something clicked in her brain—she almost heard the sound. *We do have flame!* She gripped her sword.

Before Rowan could talk her out of it, Ella opened the furnace door and set the wood inside. Then she tapped the tip of her sword against it and watched it burst into flames.

In the flickering light, Ella saw the surprised look on Rowan's face—and Jack's wide smile.

My enchantments do *matter,* she wanted to say. *And we haven't lost everything—at least not yet.*

CHAPTER 13

n the glow of the fire, Ella examined every inch of the igloo. Broken furniture. Broken plates. A jukebox left on. What had happened in here? Had someone left in a hurry—or been forced out?

One thing was for certain: her wolf was not here.

Above the din of the jukebox, she could still hear the zombie pigmen banging against the door, searching for a way in. Then she heard a piercing howl.

Ella bolted to the window and tried to wipe away the frost. "He's out there!" she cried. "Did you hear him?"

"I heard him," said Rowan. "But I'm ignoring him." She turned up the jukebox louder.

"What's wrong with you?" said Ella. "He's in trouble!"

Rowan gestured toward the door. "Well, if you haven't noticed, so are we." A *thump* from the other side sent the door vibrating on its hinges.

Ella turned away. She could see her wolf now, pacing on a narrow strip of ice. Water rushed all around him. *He's trapped on the frozen river!* she realized. But the river was so narrow. *Jump!* she called to him. *Jump to the riverbank! What are you waiting for?*

Then she saw. The riverbank was lined with snarling pigmen. Her wolf was trapped. And the ice beneath his feet was melting—fast.

"It's the pigmen!" Ella shouted to Rowan over the din of the music. "My wolf is trapped by the pigmen! He's in the river—he's so close now. We have to help him!"

She waited for Rowan to take charge—to figure out a way to fight the pigmen and get out of the igloo. But Rowan did nothing, except close her eyes and turn up the music even louder.

Ella pressed her hands to her ears. Was Rowan losing her mind? *I will too if this goes on much longer.*

She got right in Rowan's face and hollered, "How long do we wait? When will they go away?"

Rowan shrugged. "In the morning, I guess. They'll burn with the sun." She sounded oddly calm, as if she didn't care anymore—as if she could wait there forever.

Ella wanted to shake her cousin, tell her to snap out of it. But another glance out the window showed her that dawn would soon come. She saw a hint of light sliding over the horizon.

Jack pressed his face to the window, watching. "Will they burst into flames?" he asked.

Ella nodded. *Hang on,* she told her wolf. *Morning's coming.* She held her breath and waited.

Sunlight crept across the hillside, setting the snow aglow with dazzling diamonds. It crept closer . . . and closer still . . .

Jack sucked in his breath. "It's starting," he whispered. "One's burning! Yes!" He clapped his hands as a zombie pigman went down in a swirl of smoke and flames.

Ella celebrated silently, sending little *thank yous* out into the Overworld.

Then Jack lurched forward. "Wait . . . he's coming back to life!"

Ella shook her head. "It's not the same one, Jack. It can't be."

She watched as another pigman with a gold sword burned in the morning light—and then suddenly reappeared, growling and swinging his sword with rage. "It can't be," she said again under her breath. "Rowan, look at this!"

But Rowan wouldn't look. She covered her eyes and hummed along to the music.

"What's wrong with her?" Jack whispered, his eyes wide.

"I don't know," said Ella.

All she knew was that brave Rowan was crumbling before her eyes. The cousin who had vowed to protect her and Jack was suddenly the one who needed taking care of. *And I don't know how,* thought Ella. *I don't know what to do.*

She started to pace, the way Rowan would—if she were herself right now. Back and forth, back and forth, until Jack asked her to please stop.

But she couldn't stop, because the howling had started up again.

The music blared. The zombie pigmen pounded at the door. And Ella's wolf was pleading with her. *Do something!* he called to her. *Please!*

Finally, Ella walked to the jukebox and shut it off with her fist. "Jack," she said to her wide-eyed cousin, "it's time for us to fight. We've got to find a way out of here."

*   *   *

"We should use your bow and arrow," said Jack. "Because the pigmen only have swords."

Ella nodded. "Good," she said. "Now you're thinking."

If only they could get above the pigmen—climb out on the roof and shoot arrows down, like Rowan had when the skeletons were climbing toward them uphill.

Ella would have asked Rowan about that, if her cousin weren't curled up in a ball in the chair.

"Look for a way to get out to the roof," said Ella, examining the ceiling of the igloo. "Is there a crack? Anything we can make wider and climb through?"

They searched every inch, but the ceiling of the igloo was solid—thick blocks of snow built to withstand the heat of the furnace and to keep mobs out.

Ella pressed her thumbs against her forehead and thought again. "Maybe we can go *down*." She imagined digging a tunnel in the frozen ground, leading away from the igloo.

Round and round the floor she crawled, tapping here and examining there.

"What will we dig with?" asked Jack.

Ella shrugged. She hadn't thought that far ahead. "Rowan's sword maybe. It's enchanted with Sharpness."

"She lost that sword, remember?" said Jack.

Ella's shoulders slumped. "Right." For just a moment, she rested her forehead on her hands, wishing Rowan would stand up and take charge. Or that Gran were there to tell her what to do. Or that her mother could reach out from the great beyond and guide her. *Help me, Mom,* Ella whispered. *Show me how to be brave. Tell me what to do.*

"Hey!" Jack shouted. "Look what I found!" He sat beside a woven rug. Jack had slid the rug sideways, revealing something below.

A *trapdoor.*

"Jack!" said Ella, shaking his shoulder. "This could be it!"

They flung open the door and lit the passageway with a makeshift torch—another broken chair leg wrapped in flaming cloth.

"What do you see?" asked Jack.

Ella peered downward. "I'm not sure. I'm going to climb down the ladder a ways and look."

Her legs shook as she started downward. She struggled to hold on to the torch with one hand, and the rungs of the ladder with the other.

"What do you see?" Jack kept calling.

"Nothing yet!" Down she climbed, until her torch

revealed a small chamber. Something rectangular rested in the corner. A chest?

Beside it, Ella saw a round cauldron. And next to that?

She squealed. "Oh, Jack," she called upward. "You're never going to believe what I found."

"What?" He sounded so eager, Ella worried he might tumble down the ladder on top of her.

"A brewing stand, buddy. I found a brewing stand!"

CHAPTER 14

"**W**hat should I brew?"

In his oversized apron, Jack looked like a kid playing house. *Can he really do this?* Ella wondered. But she kept her worries to herself.

"Brew whatever we can use to fight zombie pigmen, Jack. You're the brew master."

He examined the ingredients lining the shelf behind the cauldron. "Nether wart," he said, plucking the red buds from a jar. "Gun powder. Glistering melon. Dragon's breath!" He named the ingredients as he selected them.

"Good," said Ella. She held the torch closer so that he could read the labels on the jars. "What can you brew with that?"

"Splash potion of healing. A *lingering* splash potion of healing."

"Great!" she said. "But . . . wait, we don't want to heal the pigmen. We want to harm them, right?"

Jack rolled his eyes. "You can't use potions of harming against hostile mobs," he said. "Those potions just make them stronger. You have to use potions of *healing*—see, those hurt zombie pigmen. Everyone knows that, Ella."

Ella fought back a smile. "I did not know that, Jack. Thank you for telling me."

She took a step backward, looking at Jack with fresh eyes. He was still just a kid, but he knew a thing or two about brewing—just like she did about enchantments. And they were going to need every potion and enchanted item they could find to get out of this igloo.

And to get to my wolf.

The thought of him stranded on the ice, mere yards away from the igloo, sent Ella crawling out of her skin. She tried not to think about it. She tried to focus on Jack's potion brewing instead.

But there was nothing she could do to help him, except wait.

While a cherry-red liquid bubbled on the stand, she held her breath. "Is it ready?" she finally asked.

"Almost," said Jack. "Hand me that bottle."

Ella did—very gently. She fought the urge to rush Jack along. But when he finally capped the bottle, she blew out her breath. "It's time then," she said. "There's only one thing left to do."

"What?" asked Jack.

"Convince Rowan to help us," said Ella.

If they were going to bust out of the igloo and fight a pack of zombie pigmen, they couldn't do it alone. They needed Rowan to help them. They had to fight together.

* * *

"Rowan, we need you," Ella said again. "Please."

Rowan sighed. "I can't. I tried to protect you, but I let you both down," she mumbled. "We lost everything—food, fuel, my map, my sword. There's nothing else I can do. I messed up."

Ella sat back. So that's what was bugging Rowan? She thought she'd let them down? "We haven't lost *everything*," Ella said, for what felt like the tenth time.

Rowan scoffed. "Right. We have a couple of enchanted weapons and a bottle of potion."

"We have more than that," said Ella. "Way more. We have each other."

When Rowan didn't respond, Ella tried again.

"We're a family," she said. "We stick together. Gran told you to protect me. And she told me to protect Jack. So that's what we're going to do—protect each other."

"I don't need—" Jack started to say.

"Shush, yes you do," said Ella. "We protect you, and you protect us too—with your potions."

Was that a flicker of a smile on Rowan's face? Ella pressed on.

"We're more than a family," she said fiercely. "We're a pack. You're my pack, and I don't want to be without you—any more than my wolf wants to be without his."

When Rowan finally turned, her eyes glistened. She heaved a great sigh. Then she said, "Okay." She held out her hand, palm down.

"Okay!" said Jack, slapping his hand on top.

"Okay," said Ella, putting her hand on theirs. She squeezed tight.

So we're really doing this! she thought, a fire igniting in her belly. *We're getting out. We're going to save my wolf. Together.*

* * *

"On the count of three," said Rowan.

She's back, Ella thought, watching her cousin arm her bow. *As strong and fierce as ever.*

Rowan held up one finger, then two.

Ella raised her sword.

"Three!"

She swung with all her might toward the wooden door and watched it burst into flames. Without missing a beat, Rowan began firing arrows through the smoke and flames. The first zombie pigman grunted and staggered backward. *Thwack! Thwang! Thwang!* With Ella's enchanted bow, Rowan fired arrow after arrow. She would never need to reload. She would keep firing until the last zombie pigman fell.

"Go!" Rowan cried. "Get out of here!"

Ella raced to the window and shattered it with her

sword. The broken shards of ice didn't catch fire, but they fizzled and smoked, sending little rivers down the windowsill.

"You first. Hurry!" said Ella, hoisting Jack through the window. He barely fit, with all the armor she had loaned him. The only armor she kept for herself was her Frost Walker boots, which she knew she would need very soon.

"Get your potion ready, Jack!"

He fell to the ground and jumped up in a flash, ready to splash any zombie who dared approach. By the time Ella crawled through, he was ready to run.

As they took off toward the river, Ella looked back at the igloo. Arrows littered the hillside, along with steaming hunks of rotten flesh. Rowan was still battling the pigmen, and she was winning.

But more pigmen lined the river, Ella knew. She could see them—feel them, bearing down on her wolf. And she was close to him now, closer than she had ever been.

Hang on, she told him. *I'm coming. Hang on.*

Jack spotted him first. "There!" he cried, pointing.

The wolf straddled a thin sheet of ice, wedged between the rocks at the river's bend. He wasn't whining or howling. He was growling, snapping his jaws at the pigmen who hovered just feet away.

"The pigmen can't get wet," Ella suddenly realized. "They can't reach him in the river. They'll drown!" But as she watched, a chunk of ice broke from beneath the wolf's paws. Any moment, the ice was going to break apart. Then her wolf might drown too. He danced sideways, whined, and gave Ella a pitiful bark.

Her heart nearly burst. Her wolf was here, in the flesh, just yards away. He *knew* her. He was calling to her. He was depending on her!

"I'm coming," she said aloud this time. "Please hold on. I'm coming!"

Ella rushed toward the river before remembering the plan. She couldn't fight off the pigmen on her own—not with only a sword by her side. She needed Jack, too.

"Are you ready?" she called to Jack.

He set his jaw and nodded, looking years older than he really was.

I hope I am too, thought Ella. *Here goes nothing.*

She took the lead, charging toward the thinnest part of the herd, where only a pigman or two stood between her and the river. Then she raised her sword and struck.

The pigman stumbled backward, his mottled skin catching fire. But Ella knew the flame wouldn't last—he would bounce back, just as the pigmen had when dawn broke this morning.

So it was Jack's turn now.

He wound back his arm, took aim, and released his splash potion—smacking the pigman in the chest. The bottle smashed, and a blanket of cherry-red bubbles rose from the frosty ground.

The pigman grunted and dropped, but the bubbles remained. "Lingering potion," Jack had called it.

This is our chance, thought Ella.

She grabbed Jack's hand and raced through the bubbles. The lingering potion of healing would strengthen them, but it would harm any pigmen who tried to follow—at least for a little while.

When she hit the edge of the stream, Ella searched for her wolf. He was downstream now, his ice raft shrinking by the second. There was no time to wonder if her Frost Walker boots would work. They *had* to work.

"C'mon, Jack," said Ella. "Time to walk on water."

She grabbed his hand again to keep him close. Then she took her first step.

The rushing river froze beneath her, step by crackly step. But just as quickly as it froze, it *un*-froze. As Ella glanced backward, she saw Jack's back foot break through the ice. He leaped forward.

"Keep up!" she called to him.

Behind Jack, the army of pigmen raged. They were determined to follow, even if it meant diving to their deaths. One after another, the pigmen charged into the river, only to be swallowed up by the rapid current.

As Ella took another step, a pigman swept past her. He grabbed her foot, tugging her down into the rushing water. Ella struggled and kicked until he finally let go.

Don't look down! she told herself. *Keep moving!*

Her wolf was only a few feet away now. Ella took another step, then another, and finally landed on the icy raft beside him.

"Get on!" she called to Jack, tugging at his arm. But he eyed the wolf warily.

"He won't hurt you!" Ella called over the rushing water. "Get on!"

As the enchanted ice beneath Jack's feet melted, he dropped, plunging into the rushing water.

"Jack!" She dropped to her knees and grabbed both of his hands. But he was so wet and heavy. His hands started to slip from her grasp.

Then she felt her wolf beside her. He crouched low and gripped Jack's cape with his powerful jaws. Together, they pulled Jack onto the ice, inch by slippery inch.

Just as the ice broke free from its rocky nest.

Side by side on that narrow strip of ice, they sailed down the river toward the falls.

CHAPTER 15

The ice raft wound around one river bend, and then another, surging faster and faster toward the falls.

"What do we do?" asked Jack.

Ella's wolf whined, panting and pacing along the narrow strip of ice. She placed her hand on the scruff of his neck to calm him.

Then she looked backward, hoping to see Rowan on the riverbank. But she could barely even see the igloo anymore. *We're on our own now,* she realized. *We have to fight.*

"Look for a tree branch to grab," she said to Jack. "Anything sticking out from the riverbank. Get low and be ready!"

But the banks of the river were clear of bush and debris. The spruce trees were too far away—much too far.

As the sound of the falls roared in Ella's ears, her wolf barked nervously beside her. He lifted his snout and howled.

"I hear you!" she cried. "I just don't know what to do!" She wrapped her arms around his neck and hung on tight.

Then an arrow whizzed across the river a few yards ahead. Ella groaned with despair.

If the falls wouldn't destroy them, the skeletons would. She reached for her bow, and then remembered that she didn't have one. Rowan had it now. *Uh-oh.*

"Jack, get down!" she cried, preparing to face the bony mobs that she knew were coming.

But that was no skeleton holding a bow on the riverbank. It was *Rowan.* And the arrow she'd shot across the water had something streaming behind it. A rope!

As the arrow struck the trunk of a spruce, the rope grew taut. Rowan held the other end. "Grab it!" she called.

Ella had only seconds to reach for the rope. It slid through one hand, burning her skin. But she caught it with her other hand—and held on.

The ice slipped beneath Ella's feet, but finally stopped moving. "Help me hold on!" she cried to Jack.

He reached for the rope. They hung there suspended for just a moment, before Rowan began tugging them and their ice raft toward the riverbank.

As Ella's wolf leaped to the safety of the riverbank, her heart swelled. *I did it*, she realized. *I protected him. I saved him!*

Rowan tugged on her end of the rope, and Ella and

Jack tugged on the other. The gap between the ice and the riverbank narrowed, and finally Jack could jump across too.

Then Ella made her final leap and fell to the ground.

She lay still for a moment, grateful for the solid earth. Then something wet and furry nuzzled her neck. Her wolf was prodding her, pushing her up—making sure she was okay.

Ella sat up, and for the first time, gazed into her wolf's eyes. She saw a wildness there, but also something familiar. She reached out her hand. "Are we friends now?" she whispered.

He licked her hand, but then stepped backward, whining. She felt his ache, his loneliness.

"You're missing your pack," she said. "I know. But we're your pack now, buddy. We're your pack now."

She reached into her pocket for the treasure she had been saving. As she offered the skeleton bone to her wolf, he took it—tentatively at first. Then he dropped his rump, settled onto the ground, and gave himself over to his treat.

"He's yours now," whispered Rowan. "It's official."

"I hope so," said Ella, reaching out to stroke her wolf's back.

But worry pricked at her heart. Would her wolf leave her the way Rowan's horse had? When it was time to go home to Gran's mansion, would he follow?

* * *

The walk back to the igloo felt like an eternity. Jack's clothes had frozen, which meant he could take only tiny steps. And his cheeks were crimson with cold. Every so often, Ella's wolf licked Jack's face, which made him laugh and kept him going.

As they neared the igloo, Ella saw immediately that something was different. Smoke curled out the chimney of the igloo. Someone had stoked the fire!

"Did you do that?" she asked Rowan, pointing toward the smoke.

Rowan narrowed her eyes and shook her head. "Let's keep our distance," she whispered. "Follow me."

They tiptoed around the igloo toward the entrance. But when they heard the whinny of a horse, Rowan began to run.

The chestnut mare stood just beside the entrance to the igloo, and she had a friend—a dappled gray horse munching on something in a bucket.

"You came back!" said Rowan, patting the mare on the neck.

She whinnied a response and nuzzled Rowan with her soft nose.

Then Ella heard someone calling from inside the igloo. And music, a melody that went straight to Ella's heart. *Gran* was inside!

She had come all this way to find them.

She had come to take them safely home.

* * *

As Ella sank into the chair by the fire, her wolf lay down at her feet. She knew now that he would definitely follow her home—he'd been glued to her side all afternoon. As he rested his chin on her foot, he let out a contented sigh.

"I know how you feel, buddy," she whispered. "We're safe now."

When Ella looked up, she caught Gran watching her with wonder.

"You're so much like your mother," Gran said suddenly—words that Ella had never heard before.

She took them in, feeling her heart swell. And as Gran took a seat and settled back, Ella waited for the story that she knew was coming.

"You're all very much like your parents," Gran said. She turned first to Rowan. "You're a warrior, like your father. And Jack, your mother was a scientist—always searching for ingredients she could blend and brew into powerful potions."

Jack sat up straight and smiled wide.

Then Gran reached for Ella's hand. "And you, my dear, are a wolf whisperer, like your mother."

Ella swallowed the lump in her throat. "My mother spoke to wolves?"

Gran nodded. "She did."

"Rowan speaks to horses!" said Jack suddenly.

Gran nodded again. "Yes, I know," she said. "Good thing, too, or I never would have found you. Your horse led me here."

Rowan's face fell. "She's not my horse," she said. "Not really."

"I know," Gran said gently. "But you'll find your horse one day."

Jack scooted forward in his chair. "Will I, too?" he asked. "Will animals talk to me?"

Gran cocked her head. "Maybe," she said. "But you have many other talents, Jack—don't you worry."

She sighed and clasped her hands in her lap. "You've all been given great gifts, just like your parents. And it was because of those gifts that they led the fight against the mobs during the Uprising. Your parents led great armies of animals that helped us fight against the mobs. They helped us *win*."

Rowan's jaw dropped. "Why didn't you tell us?" she asked. "You taught us all about enchantments and potions, but you didn't teach us the *important* things— like about our parents!"

Anger flared in Ella's chest. "Enchantments and potions *are* important things," she countered. "Don't you know that by now, Rowan?"

Her cousin sank down, looking deflated. "You're right," she finally said. "Your enchantments saved us today."

"And my potion!" said Jack.

Rowan nodded. "And your potion."

"And *your* skills with the bow and arrow," said Ella. "We fought off the pigmen together, right?"

Rowan nodded again, and gave Ella a grateful smile.

"You three make me so proud," said Gran, her voice

catching. "And I'm sorry I didn't tell you about your parents sooner. I was trying to protect you. I thought . . ." She trailed off as she picked at the frayed seam of her robes.

Then she lifted her eyes and gazed at them steadily. "I didn't think you were ready to learn the truth, but I was wrong. You *are* ready. And it's time. The pigmen you fought today are a sign, a sign that hostile mobs are growing in power. The balance is shifting, and we may need to fight—again."

A shiver of fear ran down Ella's spine, along with excitement.

"But today?" said Gran. "Today, we eat, rest, and rebuild our strength for the journey home."

"*Home*," said Rowan, savoring the word. "I'm ready."

Ella laughed out loud. "I never thought I'd hear you say that." *Just like I never thought I'd hear Gran say that I'm so much like my mother,* she thought with a rush of pride.

As Gran doled out warm slabs of her homemade bread, Jack gobbled them up greedily. He paused, with his mouth full, to ask the kind of question only Jack could ask. "Gran, are you a witch?"

Gran nearly choked on her own bread.

Of course Gran isn't a witch, Ella almost said. But she needed to hear it from Gran herself.

"Goodness, Jack. Such questions," said Gran, wiping her mouth with a cloth. "No, I'm not a witch."

He sat back, looking relieved. "Okay, but the villagers said you were."

Ella watched Gran's face change, as if a dark cloud had rolled in.

"Ahh . . ." said Gran slowly. "The villagers. Well, Jack, things aren't always what they seem. After the Uprising, some of the villagers viewed your parents as great leaders. But others saw their gifts as strange and threatening—as witchcraft. They turned against your parents, and against me."

Her voice sounded so heavy, so sad. Ella hurried over and wrapped her arms around Gran's neck, breathing in her familiar scent. "I'm sorry, Gran," she whispered.

Gran patted her arm. "It's alright, dear. We're alright now, aren't we?" She pulled back to give Ella a reassuring smile.

Ella nodded. But the wheels turned in her mind. "Wait . . ." she said slowly. "Why did the villagers turn against *you*? Gran, can you talk to animals, too?"

Gran raised a single eyebrow, the way Rowan sometimes did. Then she laughed. "There's so much I have to teach you," she said to Ella. "In time."

So she does talk to animals! Ella realized with delight. But she knew better than to push Gran for more. And as she caught Rowan's eye, Ella knew something else.

Their adventures in the Overworld, beyond the walls of Gran's mansion, had only just begun.